For Toby,
whose alter ego "Nicky Nude"
inspired the writing of this book. xx

Manufactured in Malaysia 1214 006

First Edition 2 4 6 8 10 9 7 5 3 1

Library of Congress Control Number: 2014943759

ISBN 978-1-4998-0034-0

LITTLE BEE BOOKS

An imprint of Bonnier Publishing Group

853 Broadway, New York, New York 10003

www.littlebeebooks.com

www.bonnierpublishing.com

NAKED TREVOR

Rebecca Elliott

LITTLE BEE BOOKS

Trevor was no
ordinary bird.

He was completely…

It's a well-kept secret that all birds
are actually quite naked.

Every morning they put on their feathery clothes
and go about their day.

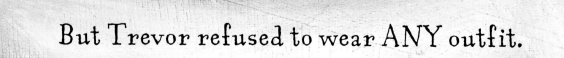
But Trevor refused to wear ANY outfit.

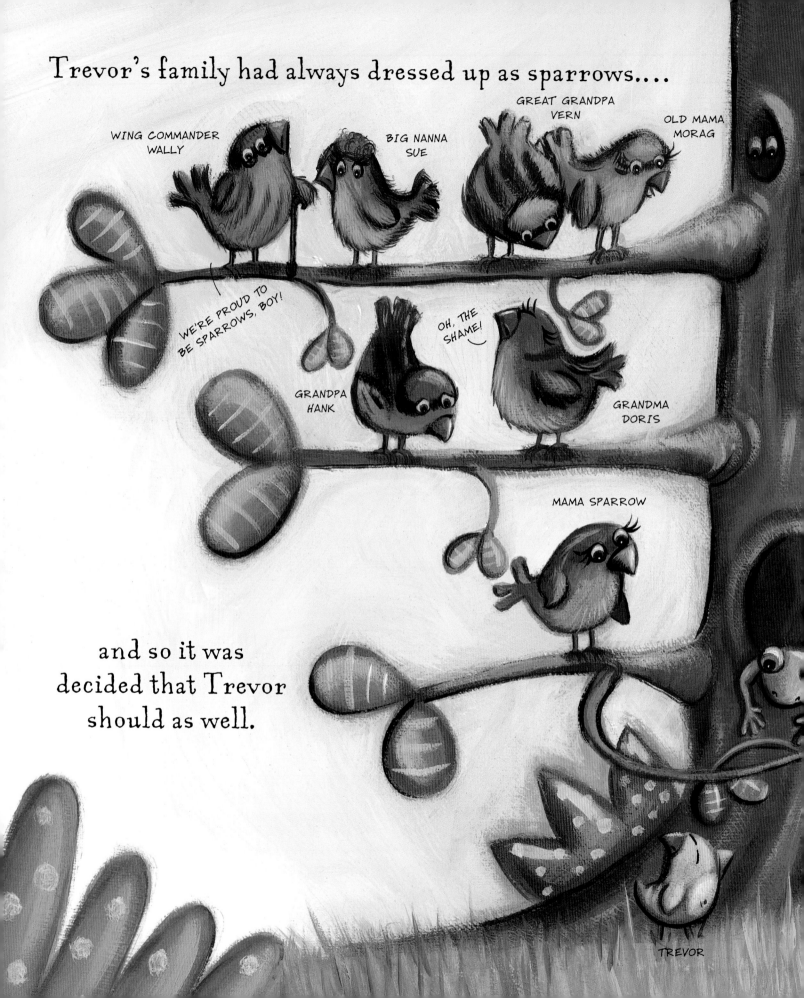

But Trevor didn't want to be a sparrow.

"You must wear your sparrow outfit!" everyone said.
"Never!" said Trevor.

Trevor wanted to find his own outfit. So one morning, he woke up very early and flew away from home.

But with no feathers on his naked wings,
Trevor wasn't very good at flying,

And so he flew...

straight into a muddy puddle.

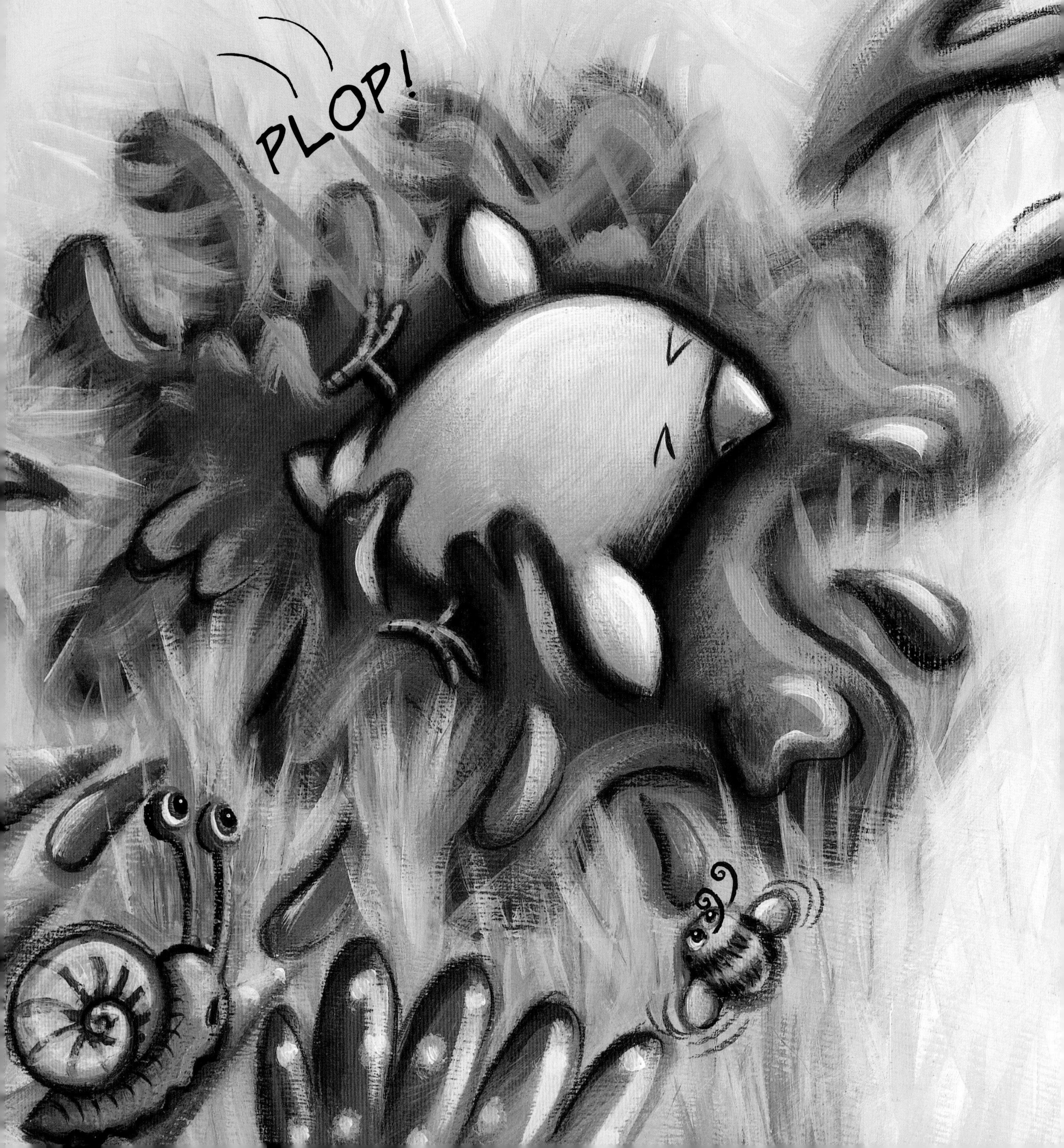

He picked himself up
and continued on his journey.

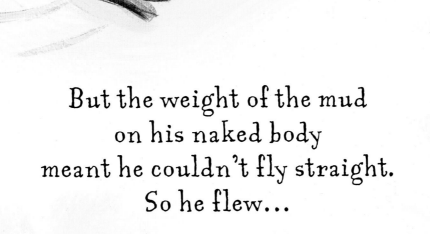

But the weight of the mud
on his naked body
meant he couldn't fly straight.
So he flew…

He picked himself up and
continued on his journey.

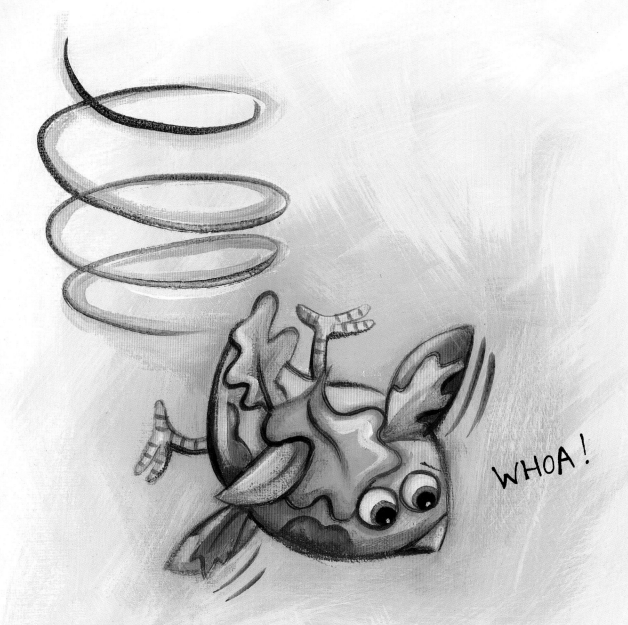

WHOA !

But the weight of the mud on his naked body
and the leaves on his naked wings
brought him spiralling down. This time he flew...

straight into a patch of beautiful flowers.

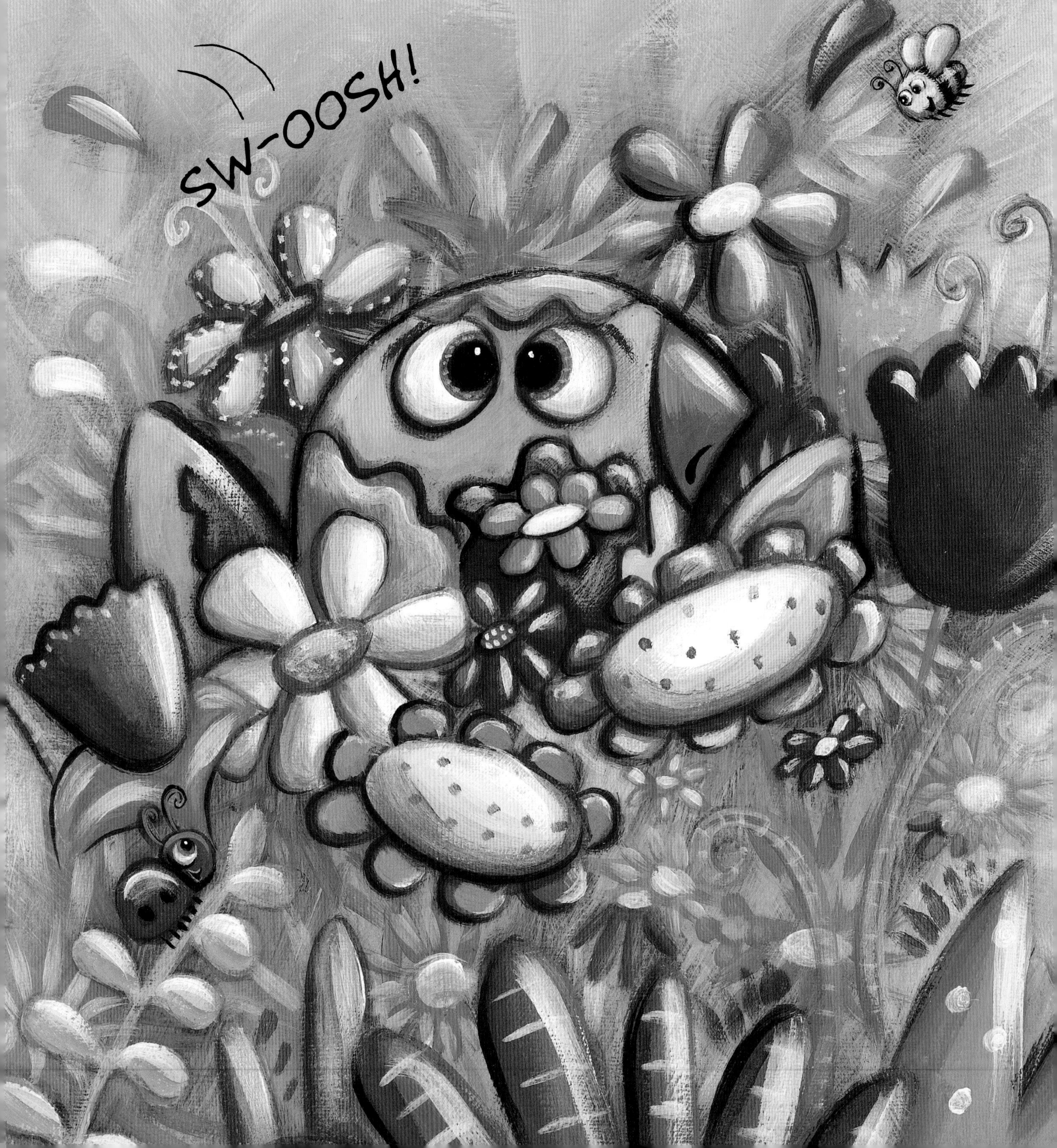

"This isn't going to work,"
Trevor said sadly.

So he launched his muddy,
leafy, flowery,
naked body into the air
and flew back home.

"OK," said Trevor,

"I'm ready to wear
my sparrow clothes now."

But everyone looked at him
and cried, "Never!"

"Why not?"
asked Trevor.

"Because you look FANTASTIC!"
they all said.

Trevor looked
down at his
beautiful new
outfit made of
mud, leaves,
and flower
petals, and he
realized that he
wasn't a sparrow
or a blackbird or
a robin. He was . . .

a spectacular
TREVOR!!

THAT'S MY BOY!

SO HANDSOME!

The others looked at their own boring
outfits and quickly took them off.

And then they were all naked.

EXCEPT for TREVOR!

THE END

FOOTBALL
Skills and Tactics

FOOTBALL
Skills
and
Tactics

EDWARD ENSOR

p

This is a Parragon book
This edition published in 2006

Parragon
Queen Street House
4 Queen Street
Bath BA1 1HE, UK

Copyright © Parragon Books Ltd 2002

Photographs © EMPICS Ltd & Getty Images
Skills photographs by Kelly Cantlon
Produced by Atlantic Publishing
Cover images © Getty Images

Cover by Talking Design

Acknowledgements
Thanks to the young footballers whose patience and skills made this book possible:
Oliver Clark; Daniel Groves; Jack Hylands; Kilara Kilama-Oceng;
Ubaid Nawaz; Richard Trafford and Corinne Hill.
Thanks also to John Dunne; Simon Taylor; Kelly Cantlon; Jane Hill; Jen Little at Empics, Richard Whiting
and Natalie Jones at Getty Images
and Watford Boys Grammar School for the use of their facilities.

A catalogue record for this book is available
from the British Library.

ISBN 1-40545-364-8
Printed in China

Contents

Introduction

Football. The World Game. The Beautiful Game. Millions of us live it and breathe it. When we're not watching our heroes, we're out there imitating them. Whether it's an organised game or just a kickabout with some friends, we all fancy ourselves as a Vieira, Owen or Beckham, maybe even a Desailly or Barthez.

If the top players have one thing in common, it's that they make difficult techniques look ridiculously easy. But we often forget that flashes of brilliance on the pitch are the result of hundreds of hours' work on the training ground. David Beckham practises free kicks endlessly so that he can come up with the goods when it matters - like that unforgettable last-minute goal against Greece which took England to the 2002 World Cup.

Every player has to start with the basics, and that means working on all the key skills until they become second nature. This book takes you through every facet of the game, step by step, breaking down the various skills and techniques into their component parts. There are plenty of tips to follow, tricks to try - and pitfalls to avoid! As well as analysing individual skills, there is also an overview of formations and tactics, emphasising the importance of attacking and defending as a team.

Each section is fully illustrated. The photographs show some youngsters putting theory into practice, while some of the game's biggest names demonstrate how it's done, even in the pressure cooker of a competitive match.

So get reading this book and then get out there sharpening those skills. The more you practise, the better player you will become. You'll also increase your understanding and enjoyment of the world's greatest game.

Warm-up

 ootballers are an impatient lot. Whether it be a kickabout in the park or a full-scale competitive match, they are always desperate to get on with the game. But wait. Football is a high-intensity sport. There will be many times during a match when you will be going flat out, and it might well happen in the first few seconds. If you are stationary and cold one minute and going at full tilt the next, you are asking for trouble.

Watch the top players getting ready to come off the substitutes' bench and you'll see that they go through a vigorous warm-up session before joining the action. This is especially important in cold weather. Youngsters aren't quite so vulnerable to muscle strains and injuries, but it is still a good idea to start copying what the professionals do before they play, just as we all like to copy their tricks on the pitch.

Jog first

And what do the professionals do? Well, before looking at any particular activities, it would help to know what you are trying to achieve. The warm-up does two important things. First, it gets the heart pumping and circulation going. Experts say that the pulse rate should be at least 120 beats per minute for optimum performance. Second, the warm-up prepares the muscles for the continuous cycle of contracting and lengthening that they will go through during the course of a game. In effect, both aspects of the warm-up have the same aims: to gear the body up for some explosive activity on the pitch and reduce the risk of injury.

A gentle jog is always a good place to start. You can build up the pace slowly, perhaps varying the stride pattern. You should work up to a flat-out sprint, by which time the heart rate will be up to the level required for optimum performance.

Stretching the quadriceps

The quadriceps is the large muscle at the front of the thigh. Adopting the position shown (left), hold your ankle and pull it towards your bottom. Make sure you are well balanced. If you need more support, the position shown on the page opposite is just as effective. Hold for twenty seconds. Repeat at least three times with each leg.

Start with a gentle jog with or without the ball.

Groin stretch
Keep the leg straight and the foot pointing ahead. It is important to keep well balanced and not to overstretch.

Lower calf

Calf

Achilles

Calf stretch

Keeping the back leg straight and the body as upright as possible, bend your front leg and move your weight forwards (left). Hold the position for twenty seconds.

Lower calf and Achilles stretch

Adopt a similar position to the calf stretch, but bend the back leg (above right and left). Keep well balanced with your weight central.

Portugal's Luis Figo stretches both his groin and hamstrings from one sitting position.

Stretching the hamstring
The hamstring is the powerful muscle at the back of the thigh. It is particularly vulnerable to tears while sprinting. Stretch one leg out in front of you while kneeling on the other. Keeping the leg straight, hold the foot and pull it towards you.

Hamstring

Stretching

When it comes to stretching, the legs naturally tend to get most of the attention. Exercises to stretch the calf muscles, hamstrings, quadriceps and groin should be carried out as a matter of course. However, loosening all the muscles is no bad thing. Stretching not only reduces the risk of injury, but also increases a limb's range of movement. Greater suppleness will be a distinct advantage during a game.

To sum up, the warm-up tends to be less important for youngsters, particularly in fine weather. But it is sensible to get into good habits early on, so make a thorough warm-up part of your pre-match routine. That way, you'll have less chance of getting caught cold when the whistle blows!

After a game or training session, it is also important to reverse the process and to 'warm down'. Ten minutes' jogging at a variable pace is ideal. Stretching all the muscle groups will also prevent them from stiffening up.

TIPS

- Jog first - only stretch warm muscles.

- Stretch gently and slowly and hold each position for twenty seconds. Never 'bounce' while stretching.

- Never overstretch. It will cause the very damage you are trying to avoid.

- Always 'warm down' after playing. Jogging and stretching are just as important at the end of a game.

An alternative way to stretch the hamstring is to sit on the floor with your leg straight then gradually move your outstretched hands towards your lower leg.

Striking the ball

AS Roma's captain
Francesco Totti scores.

The techniques for passing and shooting are almost exactly the same. Both involve striking the ball. The only difference is where you want it to end up. With a pass, your target is a team-mate; with a shot your target is the back of the net!

The ball can be struck in a variety of ways, using a number of techniques. The technique you choose will depend on the situation, and in a fast and furious game like football, the situation changes by the second. A simple sidefoot pass might be on one moment but blocked by a defender the next. Consequently, you might decide to swerve the ball around your opponent instead. It is the same with shooting. You might set yourself to drive the ball past the goalkeeper, but if he comes rushing out, you might change your mind and decide on a chip instead.

There are a lot of similarities, therefore, between passing and shooting. Indeed, it is often said that the best strikers are the ones who 'pass the ball into the net' instead of blasting it. Robbie Fowler is often singled out in this regard.

First we are going to look at some of the different techniques for striking the ball, whether be for passing or shooting. Then we can look at those two skills individually in more detail and examine the differences between them.

Techniques for striking the ball

The ball can be struck with the inside or outside of the foot, the instep, heel and even the toe on occasion. Different situations will dictate which part of the boot is used to deliver a particular pass or execute a particular shot.

The push pass

The basic sidefoot technique, where the ball is stroked along the ground, is known as the push pass. Despite its name, this technique can be used to equally good effect in front of goal - by passing the ball into the net! The inside of the foot strikes the ball at right angles to the intended direction of the pass. The large surface area of the boot that comes into contact with the ball makes the push pass very accurate and reliable over short distances. Watch any quality passing side in action and you will see countless examples of the push pass.

- The non-striking foot should be level with the ball
- Weight should be over the ball on point of impact
- The head should be steady, with eyes on the ball
- The ball should be struck through its horizontal midline

The push pass
The non-striking foot should be level with the ball as the inside of the striking foot meets the ball at right angles to the intended direction of the pass. The ball should be struck through its horizontal midline.

Holland's Patrick Kluivert with the perfect body position for a sidefoot pass.

The drive

When power and distance are required, the ball should be driven with the instep. The lofted drive is more common in long passing, since the ball can sail over opponents' heads with less chance of an interception. The low drive comes into its own when shooting for goal.

- For the low drive, place the non-kicking foot alongside the ball. Strike the ball with the toes pointing down
- Hit through the centre of the ball, and follow through
- For the lofted drive, the non-kicking foot should be slightly behind the ball. Again, toes should be pointing down on contact with the ball
- Hit through the centre of the ball, but this time below the midpoint. Follow through
- When driving the ball, either low or high, timing is much more important than brute force

The drive

The non-kicking foot should be alongside the ball. Strike the ball with the toes pointing down, hit through the centre of the ball and follow through.

Swerving the ball

Striking the ball off-centre will impart sidespin and as a result it will travel in an arc rather than in a straight line. The inside or outside of the foot can be used to swerve the ball in this way. For a right-footed player, striking the right-hand side of the ball with the inside of the foot will make it bend from right to left. This is the technique that David Beckham uses to such good effect, both in open play and from free kicks. If the same player strikes the left-hand side of the ball with the outside of the boot, it will bend from left to right.

In either case, how much will the ball swerve? Judging the amount of bend is one of the main difficulties of this technique. It will depend on the amount of pace and spin on the ball. Different types of ball and even atmospheric conditions can also have an effect.

- Practise bending the ball with the inside of the foot first, as it is easier to control
- Strike across the right-hand side of the ball about halfway up (the left side if you are left-footed)
- As your foot makes contact it should rotate slightly, wrapping around the ball
- To swerve the ball using the outside of the foot, toes should be pointing down at point of contact. The foot sweeps across the body from outside to inside, striking the ball about halfway up
- With all swerving passes, a long follow-through is important
- The above technique will result in the ball keeping low. If the ball is struck on either side but lower down, it will also swerve but it will travel higher through the air

David Beckham drives the ball and follows through.

Swerving the ball with the outside of the foot

Striking the left-hand side of the ball with the outside of the boot will bend it from left to right. Toes should be pointing down at point of contact. A long follow-through is crucial.

The volley

If the ball comes to you in the air, you have the option of controlling it or striking it first time. The advantages of the latter - the volley - are speed and surprise. Whether you are attempting to pass or shoot, striking the ball on the volley gives opponents less reaction time.

There are three main types of volley. The first two are when the ball is in front of you or to the side. The third case is when the ball is too high to reach and both feet are off the ground at the point of contact.

A controlled volley when the ball is hit before it touches the ground.

The power volley

Your head should be over the ball. With toes pointed down, strike the ball centrally using the instep. Follow through. Topspin is often generated, and this will cause the ball to dip viciously as it arcs downward.

Body position is crucial. If you are leaning back and stretching for the ball, you will get underneath it and won't be able to keep it down. That might be fine for a defender clearing his lines, but for a striker shooting for goal it would mean the ball sailing over the bar.

The power volley

• Arms outstretched for balance
• Eyes on the ball
• Head over the ball to keep it low

The side volley

Make sure you are well balanced on your standing leg. This is particularly important for a waist-high volley, when it is easy to fall away as you strike the ball. The body rotates around the standing leg as you make contact with the ball.

Strike the centre of the ball with the instep. Err on the side of making contact too high rather than too low, especially when shooting. If you get underneath the ball, it will balloon up in the air and over the bar. On the other hand, if you get over the ball, it will lose some of its pace but it still might be enough to beat the 'keeper.

The side volley

• Give yourself enough space to strike the ball

• Don't overstretch

• The non-striking foot should be in line with the ball

TIPS

The Volley:

• **The positioning of the non-striking foot is the key to a successful volley.**

• **Timing is more important than power.**

• **The follow-through is not so long as for a ground shot but a smooth action rather than stabbing at the ball is crucial.**

One of the best exponents of the volley, Eric Cantona, is completely balanced when he strikes the ball.

Timing must be perfect.

The non-kicking foot
acts as a lever.

Thierry Henry of Arsenal demonstrates the
ideal body position for the overhead kick.

Overhead kick

The kicking foot should be at full stretch. Strike the ball using the instep, with the toes curled forward. Use the non-striking leg and the arms to break your fall as you hit the ground.

Timing has to be absolutely perfect. Even the slightest error can leave you flat on your back and the ball nowhere near its target.

Heel and toe

It is difficult to control the ball using the toe of the boot, therefore this technique should be avoided whenever possible. The main exception is when going for a 50:50 ball. In such situations, stretching to toe-end the ball past an opponent might help you to retain possession. Similarly, a striker going for a loose ball with an advancing goalkeeper might toe the ball past him to score.

Accuracy using the heel of the boot is also notoriously difficult, and this technique should also be used sparingly. However, because a backheel reverses the expected direction of the pass, it can be used as a very effective surprise weapon. Strikers poaching in the box with their backs to goal usually opt to pivot and shoot or lay the ball off to a team-mate, but backheeled goals are certainly not unknown.

A variation of the backheel is using the side of the foot to play the ball behind the standing leg. Arsenal's Nwankwo Kanu is one who favours (and practises) this technique. It is especially suited to a low ball driven to the near post, and Kanu has got on the scoresheet more than once using this trick.

Even though this is the most difficult and acrobatic skill in football you must maintain complete focus on the ball.

At the point of impact the kicking leg must be straight.

The chip

Players often find themselves having to get the ball up and over an opponent (or goalkeeper!) in a restricted space. If there is too much pace on the ball, it might run out of play or go harmlessly through to the 'keeper. If space is tight and you want to hold the ball up after it lands, then the chip is the technique to use. Chipping the ball makes it rise steeply, but the backspin generated will make it 'bite' when it pitches rather than roll on. This technique can be used to excellent effect to drop the ball behind the last defender, or in one-on-one situations with an advancing goalkeeper.

- The non-kicking foot should be close to the ball, knees slightly bent
- The instep of the striking foot stabs down under the ball. It should make contact with the ball and the ground at the same time
- Minimal follow-through
- The chip is much easier with a stationary ball or one rolling towards you. It is a lot more difficult when the ball is moving away at point of contact

TIPS

Overhead kick:

- **Always practise on a soft surface.**
- **Must only be played when no opponent is close.**
- **Lean backwards before launching yourself into the air.**
- **The kicking foot should be at full stretch when contact is made.**

The chip
The non-kicking foot should be close to the ball and the instep should make contact with the ball and ground at the same time.

Passing

Joe Cole of Chelsea passes the ball. Passing is the most important skill in football.

Everyone likes to see fantastic individual skills: a mazy dribble, a flying header, a 30-yard rocket into the top corner. But statistically, these are the exceptions, not the rule. Four out of five times when an outfield player is on the ball, his next move will be to pass to a team-mate. Accurate, well-timed passing is absolutely vital to a team's fortunes on the pitch.

Manchester United and Liverpool - the two most successful British teams of the past 30 years - have had many brilliant individuals over that period. Yet managers of both clubs have always identified good passing and movement as the most important factors in their success.

Good passing requires good technique, and this has already been discussed. It also involves making the right decision at the right time.

Decisions, decisions...

A player in possession ought to have a range of passing options open to him. He has to assess all his options and decide which is the right pass to make. The game is all about getting the ball into advanced positions, and if a forward pass is on, that should be the preferred option. However, if a sideways or backwards pass means keeping possession and changing the point of attack, then these can be equally valuable.

Making such instant judgements will be greatly helped if footballers learn to play with their heads up. Indeed, good players will have an awareness of what is going on around them, even before they receive the ball.

Four out of five times when an outfield player is on the ball, his next move will be to pass to a team-mate. The sidefooted pass is usually the most effective. Height, weight, direction, and timing are the essential elements.

Sylvain Distin of Manchester City passes the ball. The weight of a pass is just as important as direction.

route. These are the riskiest passes, those most liable to be intercepted, but high risk can bring high rewards.

Weight

The weight of a pass is crucial. An underhit pass will obviously fail to reach its target. On the other hand, a pass a yard either side of a team-mate might as well be a mile wide if there is too much pace on the ball.

Direction

This will vary, depending on the circumstances. A pass straight to a team-mate will be particularly important in a congested area of the pitch, when there are opponents ready and waiting to intercept. But 'ball to feet' isn't always appropriate. In a swift counter-attacking move, for example, a pass aimed directly towards a team-mate can result in the impetus of the attack being lost. If speed merchants such as Craig Bellamy or Michael Owen are in full flight, a ball played into the space in front of them can be used to devastating effect.

Timing

Even if a pass is perfectly executed, it can go horribly astray if it is a moment too soon or too late.

Unlike with the other factors, timing is a shared responsibility between the passer and receiver. The receiver has to make himself available and ready to accept the ball, and the player in possession must deliver the pass at that precise moment. The two players may or may not make eye contact to achieve perfect timing. Team-mates who know each other very well often find themselves on the same wavelength without any obvious signal.

Height

Generally, a pass along the ground is preferable to one in the air. Passes on the deck are quicker and can be delivered more accurately. They certainly make life much easier for the receiver. Aerial passes, by definition, aren't the most direct route to a team-mate. They therefore give defenders more time to react, and that can make the difference between a successful pass and an interception.

Aerial passes can have their advantages, however. They can bypass one or more opponents who stand between the passer and the intended receiver. Long-range passing experts, such as David Beckham and Steven Gerrard, often take the aerial

TIPS

- Keeping possession is essential - a pass backwards can be a positive move.
- Practise gauging the weight of a pass. This is as important as direction.
- Look to play the ball into space for the receiving player to run on to.

The attacking player
feints to pass.

Just before contact, the player pulls back from making the
pass. It is important that all the body weight moves as if
the intended pass is going to be fully completed.

The opponent is
fully committed and out
of the play. This gives time and space to make a more
accurate pass or to move forward with the ball.

Disguise

If the player on the ball makes his intentions clear,
then he is informing his opponents as well as his
team-mates. For this reason, players should avoid
'telegraphing' their passes. A range of tricks and
techniques can be used to achieve this. Backheels
and reverse passes can be used; players can look at
one player and pass to another; dummies and feints
can help to disguise where the pass is going. A
disguised pass will give the receiver valuable extra
time on the ball.

David Beckham is challenged by Luis
Figo at a Real Madrid practice. In a game
situation there is often little time to make
decisions as pressure from opponents is
swift. Awareness of team-mates' positions
before you receive the ball is vital.

Shooting

Perfect balance from Irenio Soares of Tigres (R) shooting for Tigres during the Mexican cup final.

The old saying 'if you don't buy a ticket, you won't win the raffle' is often applied to shooting. The game is all about scoring goals, and a team that doesn't notch up many attempts is going to struggle. Good approach play is all very well, but it counts for little if there is no end product.

If the opportunity to shoot is there, go for it. Too many times you see a player with a goalscoring opportunity passing the ball - and the responsibility. Predatory goal poachers take totally the opposite view. Their first thought is to have a strike at goal, and only if there is a very low percentage chance of success do they consider other options. Such players are sometimes described as greedy, especially if their shot is saved or goes wide. But in the long run, such players will reap their rewards. You do see games where one side has a dozen unsuccessful shots on goal, while the other team has a solitary effort on target and scores. This is extremely rare, however. Statistics show that a team that gets ten or more shots on target will come out on top nearly every time. What is surprising is that, even knowing this to be true, so many players pass up perfectly good shooting opportunities.

Left: Manchester United's Wayne Rooney shoots and scores. If defenders are prepared to back off, take the opportunity to shoot.

Ole Gunnar Solskjaer playing for Manchester United. Keep your shot low. It will be more difficult for the 'keeper to save it.

Shooting checklist

Be aware. A player might miss a golden chance simply through failure to spot a good opening. This is really part of the wider theme of playing with your head up and seeing what is on at all times.

Be confident. Don't be afraid of failure. Don't turn a good shooting opportunity into a negative pass or unproductive dribble.

Be quick. Chances come and go in an instant. Players out of form and lacking in confidence are often guilty of hesitating on the ball or taking one touch too many; this can result in a good chance going begging. About half of all goals scored are with first-time shots, and that doesn't count headers, penalties and direct free kicks.

Go low. There are two reasons for this. Thundering shots into the top corner look spectacular, but they are going into the goalkeeper's favoured area. Low shots are a 'keeper's nightmare. Secondly, with a low shot even a wayward effort has a chance of a deflection, or perhaps turning into an unintended pass.

Placement versus power. For close-range shooting accuracy should come first, power second. Shots struck from distance must have power. Aim centrally. Even if the ball is heading for the middle of the goal when it leaves the boot, the slightest error, swerve or movement of the ball through the air could see it flying just inside the post once it has travelled 25 or 30 yards.

Use both feet. If defenders know you will only go for goal with your stronger foot, they will concentrate on covering that side. At one time, even Michael Owen was regarded as too one-sided. He worked on improving his shooting with his left foot, and in the 2001 FA Cup Final the Arsenal defence found to their cost how much better it had become.

Anticipate. Good strikers seem to develop an uncanny sixth sense for knowing where the ball will fall, and position themselves accordingly. Even if you haven't reached that level yet, you should be ready to gamble, for example on a team-mate winning a header or the ball rebounding off the woodwork or the goalkeeper.

TIPS

- Don't be afraid of failure.
- Regularly practise hitting the ball with your 'wrong' foot.
- Never waste an opportunity to shoot first time.
- The goal never moves, so be aware of where the target is at all times.
- Keep composed even under the pressure of a vital scoring opportunity.

Placement

Placement versus power - close to the goal, accuracy must come first.

Power

Shots from a distance must have power. Chances come and go in an instant. Be ready - half of all goals scored are from first-time shots.

England players in the wall jump to block a free kick from Artim Sakiri of Macadonia during the Euro 2004, group 7 qualifying match.

Receiving the ball

Edgar Davids playing for Holland.

assing and receiving are opposite sides of the same coin. One player's pass becomes a ball that has to be received by a team-mate. One aspect of good passing is to put the ball into an area which makes life as easy as possible for the receiver. Of course, passes that are less than perfect still have to be dealt with. Players must practise receiving a ball that might be spinning, bouncing awkwardly, travelling at great pace or coming at a difficult height.

Before the ball arrives, you should already have made up your mind whether you are going to strike it first time or bring it under control. If you are going to take the latter option, speed is of the essence. Good ball control is worth nothing in itself; it is simply a means to an end. The real end product is what you do with the ball next. Good control merely buys you extra time and space, and those valuable commodities should help to make your use of the ball that much better. Put another way, the less time you spend controlling the ball, the more time you'll have to execute your next move, be it a pass, dribble or shot.

Obviously, the fewer touches you need to bring the ball under control, the better. How often do you hear pundits and coaches referring to a player's good (or poor!) first touch. They know that the first contact between ball and body - whether it be the foot, thigh or chest - is absolutely crucial. Ball control falls into two broad categories: cushion control and firm control.

Cushion control

It is important to get the body into the right, balanced position. The ball should be cushioned by the chest so it drops to the floor by your feet. Contact should be made with the large area of the chest, which is pulled back on impact to take the pace off the ball.

Cushion control

Here, the object is to 'kill' the ball and keep it within your own playing distance. If you allow the ball to rebound a couple of yards, especially in a congested area of the pitch, what was your ball may now be a loose ball! You could find yourself having to challenge an opponent in order to retain possession.

The key point to bear in mind with cushion control is that the part of the body receiving the ball must yield on impact. A rigid, tense surface will cause the ball to rebound away from the body. Practise relaxing the muscles and withdrawing the foot (or thigh or chest) at the point of contact so as to take the pace off the ball.

Firm control

Sometimes, you want your first touch to guide the ball in a particular direction rather than kill it at your feet. An excellent example of this was Michael Owen's wonder goal against Argentina at the 1998 World Cup. The ball was played up to him by David Beckham at about knee height. Owen used the outside of his right boot to steer the ball into the space ahead of him and set up the blistering run which resulted in a stunning goal. Had he opted for cushion control, the impetus of the move would have been lost and the goalscoring opportunity may not have arisen.

Firm control
Rather than kill the ball at your feet, sometimes you want your first touch to guide it in a particular direction.

The player turns his body and makes solid contact with the ball so it bounces off in the required direction.

The ball is met by the chest, which remains firm on impact.

Firm control

Often a player will want to take a high ball on the chest and push it into the space in front of him to run on to. Here, the chest is pushed out at the point of impact.

If the ball is travelling very fast there is often no option other than to keep the body solid on impact and guide it down to the ground. Here it is important to get well on top of the ball.

Alan Shearer of Newcastle United guides the ball into his path using his chest. It takes a lot of practice to gauge how much pace to take off the ball.

Controlling the ball

Sole of the foot.
Trapping the ball this way will bring it to a standstill. It requires perfect timing to ensure the ball doesn't bounce off the foot or slide underneath it. The position of the foot is the same as for a sidefoot pass or trap.

Getting in line

Whether you opt for cushion or firm control, the same principles apply. Decide which part of the body you're going to use to receive the ball as early as possible. Get your body into line with the ball. Go and meet the ball, don't wait for it to arrive. Use your body to shield the ball from your marker. Keep your eyes on the ball, but don't watch it all the way. The reason for this is that if you are concentrating 100 per cent on controlling the ball, then you can't be giving any thought to what you are going to do with it! Instead, try to glance around you or use your peripheral vision while the ball is on its way. You must be aware of what is going on around you before the ball arrives.

Occasionally, even the best players get the balance all wrong between controlling the ball and thinking about what they are going to do with it next. With a straightforward pass and no pressure from an opponent, it is sometimes easy to concentrate too much on your next move and forget about controlling the ball!

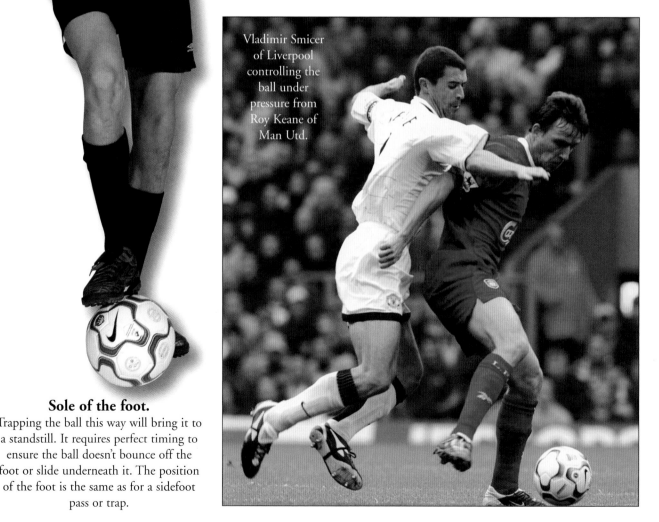

Vladimir Smicer of Liverpool controlling the ball under pressure from Roy Keane of Man Utd.

Controlling the ball

◀ Top of the foot.
Only used when a ball is
dropping from a height.
The ball should be
cushioned as the foot
drops to the floor with
the ball.

▲ Front of the foot.
This is only a last resort
when it is impossible to get
into the correct position
with the side of the foot.
With less surface area in
contact with the ball, there
is more room for error, with
the ball glancing off at an
angle or too far away.

Side of the foot. ▲
This is the most popular
and most effective way to
bring the ball under
control. The broadest
area of the foot comes
into contact with the
middle of the ball,
bringing it to rest just in
front of the player. The
leg should be moved back
along the line of the ball's
flight so as to take the
pace off the ball and
bring it to rest in the
required position.

▲ Thigh control.
Lower the leg so as to cushion it as the ball
makes contact. This will bring the ball to
rest at your feet rather than cause it to
bounce out of control.

To sum up, good control can be the difference
between retaining and losing possession,
exploiting an attacking opportunity or missing
out. Top players are often praised for their
ability to find time and space, even in the
tightest games. These will invariably be players
whose ball control is excellent.

Ruud van Nistelrooy
of Manchester United
shields from William
Gallas of Chelsea.

When you have possession keep your body between your opponent and the ball and stand your ground while using your body strength against the defender as he pushes into you. Good balance is essential.

You can screen the ball to block any attempt by your opponent to get around you. Keep the ball close to you. If the ball is well away from your body, beyond your playing distance, blocking an opponent in this way would be deemed obstruction and result in a free kick.

TIPS

- Once you sense a defender at your back try to keep him guessing as to which way you will turn.

- Shielding the ball can create valuable time for your team-mates to give you support and options for passing.

- If your opponent is close to you consider the option of leaning into him and rolling your body against him to make a turn. This is a particularly good option when you only need to gain a small amount of space for a shooting opportunity.

Shielding the ball

Sometimes you will have the luxury of being able to receive the ball or play it while in plenty of space. More often you will have an opponent closing you down and looking for an opportunity to challenge. This is when screening or shielding the ball comes into its own. Quite simply, the golden rule is to keep your body between your opponent and the ball, thereby making it much more difficult for him to make a tackle without committing a foul.

If you receive the ball with a defender close at hand, you should use your first touch to steer the ball away from him. This assumes, of course, that you are aware of the defender's presence in the first place! A quick look while the ball is on its way to you will ensure this. You will see from the above examples that protecting the ball gains you time and should help you to use it more productively.

Dribbling

Cristiano Ronaldo of Manchester United is one of the best dribblers in the Premiership.

There is no set dribbling skill as such. Any move that takes a player past an opponent while keeping possession of the ball comes under the dribbling banner. Players tend to develop highly individual methods of beating a player, though there are some common features which can be observed again and again.

Dribbling is a risky business. Even the very best - someone like Cristiano Ronaldo - will run out of luck eventually. Better to dribble past one player and put in a good pass than to beat three players and lose the ball to the fourth.

Because of the risks involved, dribbling is best confined to the attacking third of the pitch, particularly when defenders are back in numbers and everyone is tightly marked. In such circumstances, going past one defender will force another to come and challenge for the ball. That defender might well leave a team-mate unmarked and space to exploit.

When to dribble

Dribbling in midfield, defence - or, in Fabien Barthez's case even in your own penalty area - is a very dangerous game. When Barthez cleverly takes the ball past a striker it looks brilliant and brings cheers from the fans. But there have been occasions when he has lost possession, with disastrous results. In those situations, there is no way a 'keeper or his team-mates can recover and a goal is a near certainty.

Feinting

Feinting is an important part of the dribbler's art. It involves fooling your opponent into thinking you are going to go one way, then moving off in a completely different direction. You can do this in a lot of ways, but the common element in all cases is the use of exaggerated body movements.

Successful dribbling

Keep the ball under close control.

Kicking the ball too far ahead will make the defender's job easy.

Keep your head up.

It is important to be aware of where your team-mates and opponents are at all times.

Attack with pace.

A striker running at pace with the ball under control is a defender's nightmare. If you haven't got the blistering turn of speed of a Michael Owen or Ryan Giggs, then change of pace can be equally effective.

Change direction.

Constant twisting and turning is a sure way to keep a defender on his toes. The more often he has to adjust his stride pattern, the more chance you have of putting him off balance.

Shield the ball.

Always try to keep your body between the defender and the ball. This will make it far more difficult for your opponent to dispossess you without committing a foul.

Use feints and dummies.

This is a big subject all by itself. In short, you pretend to do one thing and do another. This covers any movement which sends your opponent in one direction while you speed off in another.

Use both feet to play the ball.

Most players have a stronger leg, but if you always use that one to play the ball, the defender will use that knowledge to his advantage. Similarly, don't try to beat a defender on the same side every time. The more you can keep your opponent guessing, the better your chances will be of getting past him.

1.
As you approach the defender, transfer your body weight to the left to make it look as if you are going to move in that direction.

3.
Push off this foot and go past your opponent on the left, playing the ball with your left foot as you do so.

Dropping the shoulder

As you might expect, this is primarily an upper-body feint.

2.

An exaggerated drop of your left shoulder fools the defender into thinking you plan to go that way.

3.

As the defender reacts, swerve the other way and accelerate past him on the right.

2.

Instead, swing your foot over the ball and plant it on the ground.

The step-over

1.

Make as if to play the ball with the outside of your right foot.

The dragback

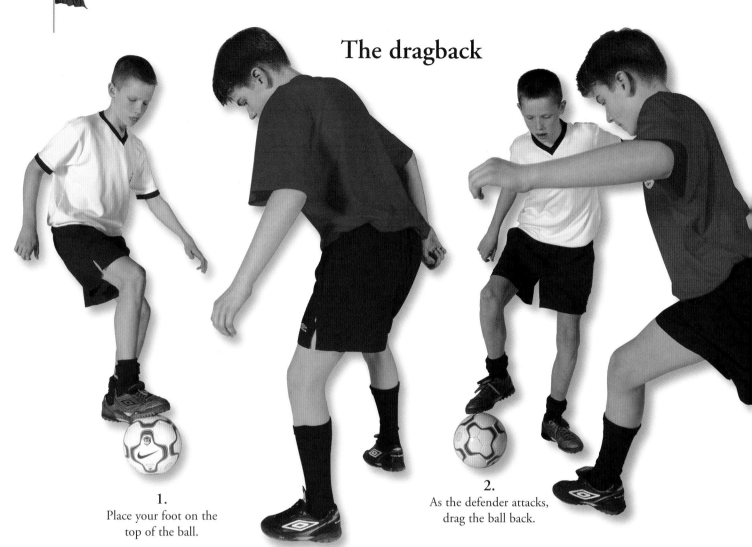

1.
Place your foot on the
top of the ball.

2.
As the defender attacks,
drag the ball back.

Robert Pires of
Arsenal is a master
of the dragback.

The dragback

This is when the attacker uses the sole of the boot to draw the ball back and reverse the direction of play. It is particularly effective if you are running alongside a defender at pace. As you suddenly stop and drag the ball back, the defender sails past you and, for the moment at least, he is no longer a threat. Former World Footballer of the Year Zinedine Zidane is one player who has perfected the double dragback. As he completes the first trick with one foot, he pivots and does a second dragback using the other. As this involves two rapid changes of direction, it is quite bamboozling for defenders. It is also very difficult to do! Practise the single dragback before you even think about trying this one.

Feinting

Feinting is an important part of the dribbler's art. It involves fooling your opponent into thinking you are going to go one way, then moving off in a completely different direction. You can do this in a lot of ways, but the common element in all cases is the use of exaggerated body movements. Defenders are supposed to concentrate on the ball, not on the movement of the body.

Dribbling practice:

· **Use the inside and outside of both feet.**

· **Don't kick the ball too far ahead of you. Good control means keeping the ball within your playing distance at all times. A lot of light taps of the ball will achieve this; a few heavy ones won't!**

· **Don't concentrate so much on the ball that you aren't aware of the position of the next cone (or, if it were a game, the next defender!). Play with your head up.**

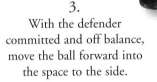

3.
With the defender committed and off balance, move the ball forward into the space to the side.

Mark Kennedy practises dribbling using cones.

However, you will find that even the best defenders will react to body movements. Trying to fool a defender in this way is also known as 'selling a dummy'. If the defender follows the body movement when he shouldn't have, he is said to have 'bought the dummy'. There are many variations. Watch players like Harry Kewell, Robert Pires and Ryan Giggs in action and see how they adapt the basic techniques to their own personal style. Then why not experiment with a few ideas of your own?

Practising

One of the simplest and best ways of practising your dribbling skills is to weave in and out of a set of cones. You can place the cones in a variety of ways to make up a slalom course. Space them fairly wide apart at first, as these will be easier to negotiate. As you improve, you can bring them closer together. This will make the turns a lot tighter and really test your close control.

Tackling and defending

Didier Drogba of Chelsea is tackled by Ledly King of Tottenham Hotspur.

Only challenge for the ball when you feel confident of winning it. Jockey for position while you are waiting for the right moment to strike.

There is a lot more to defending than just tackling. Tackling covers the techniques you can use to try to win the ball from an opponent. Defending is a much wider subject. It involves decision-making and taking up positions which will help you win the ball or prevent your opponents from using it to good effect. Let's look at the two aspects separately.

Tackling

You should challenge for the ball when you feel confident of winning it. Watch the ball, not any feints or dummies that your opponents might throw. Conversely, if you feint to tackle, it might force the error or opening you are looking for. Jockey for position while you are waiting for the right moment to strike. This includes using your body position to manoeuvre your opponents into less dangerous areas.

When you decide to make a tackle, the important factors are speed, determination, accuracy and timing. If either of the first two factors is lacking, then you have less chance of winning possession. If you tackle clumsily or get your timing wrong, you run the risk of fouling your opponent and conceding a free kick.

Right: Heskey of Birmingham City perfectly timing his tackle on Bocanegra of Fulham.

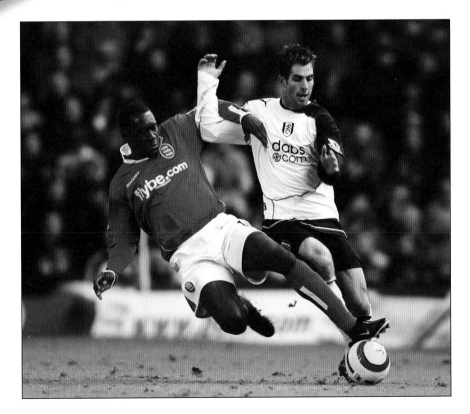

The block tackle

The block tackle is the most common challenge in football. It can be made from the front or the side, but in both cases the side of the foot is used to block the ball. If both players meet the ball at the same time, it isn't necessarily the biggest or strongest player who will come away with it. Indeed, you only have to look at players such as David Batty to see that the lower centre of gravity of shorter players can be a distinct advantage.

In a front-on tackle you should put your standing foot beside the ball and lean into the challenge with your full body weight driving through the tackling leg. If you are running alongside an opponent when making a challenge, you will have to pivot on your standing foot so as to bring your tackling leg round into the block position. This is obviously a weaker tackle since your body weight isn't behind the ball.

When you arrive at the ball at the same time, first ensure a good body position with your weight over the ball.

To win the ball, you must get as much of your foot in contact with it as possible. Your full body weight should drive through the tackling leg.

On contact, push the ball up and over the top of your opponent's foot.

The slide tackle

Generally speaking, you should always try to stay on your feet. Once you go to ground, even if it is only for a couple of seconds, you are out of the game. You should therefore only commit to such a tackle if you are certain of winning the challenge, or if the situation is desperate, for example when a striker is through on goal.

Most sliding tackles are made from behind. The defender must make sure he does not make contact with the attacker's leg first or he will concede a free kick. The defender will have more chance of making a clean challenge if he tackles with his outside leg, the one furthest away from the player in possession. This also gives a stronger tackling position. In practice, however, even the best defenders tend to tackle with their stronger leg, no matter which side of the opponent they are on.

It isn't too difficult to win the ball using a slide tackle; winning possession isn't quite so easy. If the timing is perfect, you can hook your foot round the ball and cradle it there throughout the tackle. As the attacker rides over the defender's leg, the latter gets up with the ball at his feet. More commonly, the slide tackle is used simply to dispossess an opponent. The ball might be knocked out of play, or into space for a team-mate to try to pick up possession.

Maccabi Haifa's Eitan Azaria puts in a sliding tackle on Valencia's Vicente (L)

Never make the tackle from too far behind your opponent.

If the timing is perfect, you can hook your foot round the ball and cradle it there throughout the tackle.

Defending

It is important to remember that defending is not the sole preserve of defenders. When the opposition are in possession, every player is a defender. Good teams defend from the front. That means that strikers - who can be regarded as the first line of defence - should be the first players to pressure the ball. There may be one or two strikers up against three or four defenders, so the striker may not get a tackle in. However, strikers can deny defenders time and space, cut down their options and maybe hurry them into making a mistake.

It goes without saying that a defender must be goalside of the player on the ball if he is to close him down or make a challenge. Apart from tackling, there are other defenders' tricks you can employ to minimise the danger and help to win possession back for your team.

Interceptions. Be alert for an underhit or misdirected pass. If you can steal the ball before it reaches the intended receiver, you won't need to tackle him.

Prevent your opponent from turning. A player receiving the ball will pose a greater attacking threat if he is allowed to turn. The defender should react quickly and aim to get within three feet of his opponent by the time the ball reaches him. If you lay off much further, the attacker will have room to set

Spain's youth international Juanfran (L) gives himself room to see the ball and tries to steer the attacker, Josh Simpson of Canada, away from the danger area.

Prevent your opponent from turning
Get close to the attacker but not too close. Here (left) the defender's view of the ball is restricted and a quick move from the attacker could take him out of range before the defender has time to react.

himself to pass, dribble or shoot. If you get too close, it will be difficult to keep the ball in view, and a quick move from the attacker could take him out of range before you have time to react.

Force your opponent into a less dangerous area. If a defender can force his opponent towards the touchline or across the field, he can break down the impetus of an attack. He will also be buying time for his team-mates to get into optimum positions, covering any forward passing options.

Jockey and be patient. Even if the attacker has been able to turn, the onus is still on him to do something with the ball. The longer he retains possession, the more chance he has of making a mistake. Don't dive in unnecessarily and solve his problem for him. Bide your time and wait for a momentary loss of control, when the odds will be stacked in your favour.

The Women's League Cup: Fulham v Arsenal. Generally speaking, when defending, you should always try to stay on your feet. Once you go to ground, even if it is only for a couple of seconds, you are out of the game.

Heading

Frank Lampard of Chelsea jumps
to head over Gary Kelly of Leeds.

ootball purists often say that the game is meant to be played on the deck, not up in the air. They don't like to see a lot of aerial ping-pong. But sometimes a high ball is exactly the right option to choose. Once the ball is in the air, both teams will want to challenge for it. If you wait for the ball to drop, you run the risk of losing possession, or maybe even conceding a goal. No matter what the purists say, heading is a skill that can win and lose games.

Statistically, about 20 per cent of goals are scored from headers. That figure went up to 66 per cent in the 1998 World Cup Final, when two of the three goals which brought France victory came from the head of Zinedine Zidane. The former World Footballer of the Year is acclaimed as one of the game's great artists with the ball at his feet, but it was his prowess in the air that helped beat Brazil on that occasion.

Heading a ball doesn't come naturally. You can often see toddlers happily kicking a football around, but you won't see them readily engaging in heading practice. We seem to go into automatic self-preservation mode when we see an object hurtling towards our face. This defensive reaction usually involves closing the eyes and turning away - the very things you shouldn't do!

There are four main points to bear in mind when heading the ball:

Use the forehead.
This is a relatively flat surface and will make controlling the direction of the header easier. The skull is at its thickest here, and even a firmly struck ball won't hurt. Finally, by making contact with the ball above the eyes you will be able to watch the ball right up to the moment of impact.

Keep your eyes open.
Many still photographs show that even professionals close their eyes at the precise moment of contact between head and ball. This is quite normal. However, you should try to keep your eyes on the ball for as long as possible.

Attack the ball.
Be positive. Go to meet the ball, don't let it hit you. This isn't just a matter of technique. If you wait for the ball to come to you, the chances of an interception are greater.

Robbie Keane of Tottenham and Paul Reid of Brighton battle for a header.

Arch your back, nod your head

In many cases, you will be trying to get maximum power into your header. By arching your back and snapping forward at the point of contact, you will give your head forward momentum when it meets the ball. Even more power is generated if you also use your neck muscles to punch through the ball at the same time.

To put all four of these key points into practice with a moving ball is a tall order. Much better to work on good technique with a static ball first. The easiest way to do this is to suspend a ball at a suitable height. When you are timing your headers well in this way, you can move on to heading balls thrown gently by a partner.

Titus Bramble of Newcastle beat Tierry Henry of Arsenal to a header.

Defensive header

Keep your eyes open and watch the ball right up to the moment of impact. Use your arms for leverage, but if they are too high it is easy to give away a free kick. For a defensive header you should try to make contact below the horizontal midline of the ball. Too high and you'll head the ball down, possibly to an attacker; too low and the ball will go up into the air but won't travel far.

Different types of header

Defensive header. Here, you are aiming for maximum power and distance. Direction is less important, though it is generally better to put the ball out wide rather than down the middle. If your header finds a team-mate, that's a bonus.

You should try to make contact below the horizontal midline of the ball. Too high and you'll head the ball down, possibly to an attacker; too low and the ball will go up into the air but won't travel far.

Heading for goal. In this case, accuracy is obviously far more important than with a defensive header. Remember that a downward header poses most problems for a goalkeeper. You therefore need to make contact with the ball just above the horizontal midline.

If you are meeting a cross, you have two choices. One is to make a fuller contact and aim for the near post. This is sometimes described as heading the ball back the way it has come. The other option is to use the pace of the ball and deflect it off your forehead towards the far post. Judging the exact angle of deflection isn't easy - but then, it won't be easy for the defenders or goalkeeper to anticipate either.

Cushioned header. If a defender is passing back to his goalkeeper, or a player is trying to set up a team-mate, too much pace on the ball can be a major headache. In such cases, you should relax the back and neck muscles. Instead of generating power, you will take a lot of the pace off the ball and make life much easier for the receiver.

Attacking header
A downward header poses most problems for a goalkeeper. Contact with the ball for an attacking downward header should be just above the horizontal midline. Be positive. Go to meet the ball, don't let it hit you. Statistically, about 20 per cent of goals are scored from attacking headers.

An attacking header from Paul Scholes .

TIPS

- Meet the ball, don't let it hit you. If you head the ball properly it won't hurt you.

- Keep your eyes on the ball at all times.

- Where possible head from a standing position for better balance.

- As the head goes forward the arms go back and down for leverage. Take care with the elbows.

Goalkeeping

Fabien Barthez confidently
collects a high ball.

As the last line of defence, goalkeepers can be the hero or villain of the piece, and sometimes both in the same game! Brilliant saves can win matches; blunders are nearly always punished.

Most people regard Peter Schmeichel as the number one 'keeper of the past decade. At his peak, Schmeichel was said to be worth 10 points a season to his team, and that can be the difference between champions and also-rans.

Dominating the penalty area

Speed, agility, lightning reactions and excellent handling skills are some of the obvious qualities required to be a good goalkeeper. There is much more to the art, however. Goalkeepers have to be brave, prepared to go for the ball when the strikers' boots might be flying. The best 'keepers dominate their penalty area, both physically and with a powerful set of lungs! A decisive, commanding 'keeper makes defenders' lives much easier. Schmeichel and other top performers can be seen constantly bawling at their team-mates. This is crucial, as they are invariably best placed to spot any danger signs early on. Commanding 'keepers instil confidence in the outfield players, and strong defences are built on confidence, just as much as technical ability and good positional play.

The other quality that must be mentioned is concentration. Goalkeepers may have nothing to do for long periods, then find themselves facing a high-pressure one-on-one situation. It is vital for 'keepers to stay focused on the game at all times.

Be ready and stay well balanced on the balls of your feet - not on your heels. Keep your legs slightly bent.

Goalkeeper Pat Onstad of the San Jose Earthquakes stops a penalty. Speed, agility, lightning reactions and excellent handling skills are the essential qualities to be a good goalkeeper.

Shot stopping.

Goalkeepers should try to get as much of the body as possible behind the ball. Two hands are therefore better than one, and if the body is behind the hands to provide a second barrier, so much the better. Of course, this isn't always possible and getting anything behind the ball is important. This might be a hand, the fingertips, even an outstretched leg.

Shots along the ground.

For shots along the deck most 'keepers tend to drop one knee to the ground and scoop the ball up with both hands. Others bend their backs and stoop to take the ball. Although this is a matter of individual preference, the former technique is safer and should certainly be adopted if conditions are poor or the pitch is bumpy.

Low shots.

For shots between knee and waist height, get the body behind the ball and use the scooping technique to bring it into the chest. If the shot is low, the body will naturally topple forward, but the ball will be safely cupped to the chest before you hit the ground.

Shots at chest height.

These are bread-and-butter saves, as the ball is going exactly where you want it. Two techniques are commonly used. One is to cup the hands around the ball as it hits the chest. The body should yield on impact to provide a cushioned surface and help the ball 'stick'.

Shots at chest height or straight at the 'keeper are bread-and-butter saves.

Diving low to one side

When it is impossible to get the body completely behind the ball it is particularly important to watch the flight of it and catch it with the palms facing down.

However, the danger with this technique is that the ball may rebound off the body before the keeper has clutched it. For that reason, some 'keepers prefer to catch the ball out in front of the body. Here, the fingers are spread and pointing upwards. The hands 'give' as the ball is taken.

Diving

If the ball is high and to the side try to push off with the leg nearest the ball and aim to get both hands on it if possible. If you can only reach the ball with one hand, make contact with the open palm and outstretched fingers. Guide the ball over the bar or round the post.

Taking high balls.

Catch the ball at the highest possible point. The lower it drops, the more vulnerable you will be to a challenge. Maximum height will be gained with a one-footed take-off. This has a secondary advantage, for the leading leg will give a measure of protection. The fingers should be spread wide and not too tense. Once the ball is in the hands, bring it down to the chest as soon as possible.

Diving.

For shots wide of the 'keeper, where he is unable to get his body behind the ball, he may have to launch himself to make a save. Push off with the leg nearest the ball and aim to get both hands on it if possible.

Catch or punch?

Catching the ball is always the preferred option, as long as it can be done safely. A mistimed punch could land the ball straight at an attacker's feet, while a deflection over the bar or round the post means conceding a corner. If a 'keeper is under pressure - contesting a high ball with a tall striker, for example - a punch might be the better choice. Some goalkeepers use one clenched fist, others two, but the object is always to get maximum height and distance. Putting the ball out on to the flanks is safer than keeping it in a central position. Similarly, for a shot dipping under

the bar or going just inside the post, a deflection is often a better percentage save than a catch, and it may be your only option. To deflect the ball, make contact with the open palm and outstretched fingers. Guide the ball over the bar or round the post. Take care not to get too full or firm a contact, as this might keep the ball in play in a dangerous area.

Antti Miemi tries to get two hands to the ball in this full-length dive.

Tipping the ball over the bar.
If the ball is too high to catch or too risky to punch, deflect the ball over the bar. This can also be an effective way of dealing with crosses

Positional play

Goalkeepers ought to be constantly adjusting their position depending on where the ball is. In theory, the 'keeper should place himself so that he is in a direct line between the ball and the centre of the goal.

As well as moving to the left or right, the goalkeeper also has to be ready to go forward. If an attacker is through on goal, the 'keeper must aim to make himself as big an obstacle as possible. At the same time, he will be restricting the attacker's view of the goal. Narrowing the angle is a vital weapon in the 'keeper's armoury, but it isn't a risk-free option. If he advances too far or not far enough, too soon or too late, he will hand the initiative to the attacker, who might pass, dribble or go for a chip. The 'keeper should advance quickly when the ball is outside the attacker's playing distance. When the attacker has the ball under close control, the 'keeper should check his movement and take up a ready position.

Good positioning can make difficult saves look relatively easy. Indeed, 'keepers who are repeatedly having to make spectacular saves may be guilty of poor positional play. Being in the right place at the right time is perhaps the most important aspect of the goalkeeper's art, and probably the most difficult to learn. Good judgement comes with experience.

Albacete's goalkeeper Manuel Almunia catches the ball. This is always the preferred option, as long as it can be done safely.

Always make sure you have a good view of the ball. From free kicks it is often best to get a good view of your opponent kicking the ball rather than have your vision completely obscured by the defending wall.

Distribution

Finally, the importance of the goalkeeper as an attacking player should not be underestimated. Once he has claimed the ball, he should be alert to the attacking possibilities in front of him. A long throw or kick can quickly turn defence into attack. If the opposition have poured forward in numbers, the 'keeper can take several players out of the game with a well-directed throw or kick.

Once again, Schmeichel is a past master at this art. His quick thinking has produced many goals over the years.

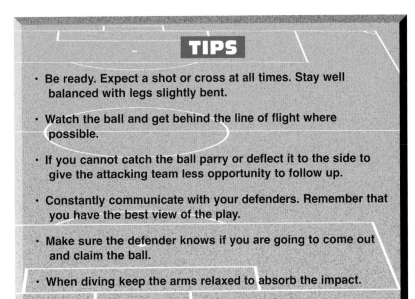

TIPS

· Be ready. Expect a shot or cross at all times. Stay well balanced with legs slightly bent.

· Watch the ball and get behind the line of flight where possible.

· If you cannot catch the ball parry or deflect it to the side to give the attacking team less opportunity to follow up.

· Constantly communicate with your defenders. Remember that you have the best view of the play.

· Make sure the defender knows if you are going to come out and claim the ball.

· When diving keep the arms relaxed to absorb the impact.

Attacking from set pieces

early half of all goals come directly or indirectly from set plays. No team can afford to ignore such a rich source of goal supply. Throw-ins, corners, free kicks and penalties have two major advantages. First, the player taking the kick or throw is dealing with a stationary ball and is under less pressure. Second, set pieces can be rehearsed and refined on the training ground. Your team-mates know exactly what is going to happen - where they have to move, whether they will receive the ball or be a decoy runner - and this gives you an important edge over your opponents.

You might be thinking that if set pieces are so productive, a team should go all out to create as many of them as possible. In practice, they tend to be a spin-off from good attacking play. A goalkeeper might turn a shot round the post for a corner; a defender might concede a penalty with a desperate challenge on an attacker through on goal; a full-back's slide tackle on a winger might give away a throw-in. In all of these situations the attacking side would have preferred to keep the ball in play; the set piece is a second-best option.

Apart from good attacking play, the best way of generating set piece opportunities is to pressure the ball when your opponents, particularly defenders, are in possession. Defenders under pressure are more likely to put the ball out of play or concede free kicks.

Free kicks

Of all set plays, free kicks produce the greatest number of goals. When it comes to deciding whether to shoot (assuming that it's a direct free kick), the distance from goal and the angle will be the critical factors. If the kick is too wide or too far out, then your aim should be to get the ball into the danger area. Generally, that means playing the ball behind the last defender. Defenders like to play the ball in front of them; they hate turning and having to defend while facing their own goal, particularly if they are under pressure.

Electing to shoot.

For more central free kicks which are within striking range, the defending side has even more to worry about. They will usually put up a wall to give the goalkeeper extra protection. Of course, the attacking side has the initiative, and a chip or pass could take all the defenders in the wall out of the game. Having said that, most teams who get a direct free kick just outside the box will usually elect to shoot. This is because the 'move' involves just one touch from one player. As a rule, the more elaborate the free kick - that is, the more players and touches it involves - the more chance there is that it will go wrong.

Play to your strengths.

Not all sides have a David Beckham in them. Play to your own team's strengths. If you have a player who is good at bending the ball, by all means use him. If you have someone with an explosive low drive, then you could set him up by playing the ball square. The same applies if you have players who are particularly strong in the air or who are good at timing their runs into the space behind the defence. The latter cases all involve at least two players and two touches and therefore will be particularly useful for indirect free kicks.

One final word. It is always a good idea to have two or three players lined up to take a free kick. Your team will know what is going to happen, but dummies and decoys will create confusion and uncertainty in the defence.

David Beckham is one of the world's best strikers of a dead ball. He has scored many goals for Real Madrid and England from free kicks.

Corners

A team can expect to be awarded several corners during a game and these can be a rich source of goalscoring opportunities. Some types of corner offer a greater chance of scoring than others.

Corners may be subdivided in terms of the distance the ball travels (near post, middle of the goal or far post) and the angle of delivery (inswing or outswing).

As far as the distance is concerned, near-post corners are the most difficult to defend against. The further the ball travels, the more time the 'keeper and defenders have to react. The near-post attacker might go for goal himself with a glancing header or flick the ball on to a team-mate.

One variation guaranteed to retain possession is the short corner. By some quick passing or maybe a dribble, the attacking side might be able to deliver the ball into the box from much closer in, from a different angle, or both.

Inswing or outswing?

The advantage of outswinging corners is that they are swerving away from the goalkeeper and defenders. The attacking players will be meeting the ball and this can help to generate a lot of power on a header or shot. Inswinging corners may be going towards the 'keeper but it will be in a very congested area. The slightest touch, either by an attacker or defender, can produce a goal.

Of all the permutations, inswinging near-post corners have been shown to produce most goals. Coaches know this, of course, and there will always be near-post defenders guarding against that type of ball. The corner taker must try to avoid the first defender with his delivery.

Luis Figo of Portugal takes an inswinging corner.

Throw-ins

In defensive positions the throw-in tends to be used simply to restart the game and retain possession. In the attacking third, it can be a formidable weapon. Many teams have a long-throw expert capable of reaching the near post, making this set piece as valuable as a corner. Even if you can't achieve such distances, you can still increase the attacking threat by bearing in mind the following points:

- The thrower should have more than one option. If players are on the move, some perhaps making pre-planned dummy runs, then space can be created for the receiver.

- If the marking is tight, the thrower is often the free player. He should make himself available for a return pass as soon as he has taken the throw.

- Make life as easy as possible for the receiver, just as you would with any other kind of pass. Your team-mate won't appreciate a ball bouncing awkwardly in front of him, or delivered where his marker can get in a challenge.

- Be ready to exploit space. A ball thrown into space beyond a defender could set up a team-mate to cross or shoot. Remember, there is no offside from a throw-in so the attacker can make his run early.

- Quick throw-ins are more likely to catch defences out, and the nearest player should therefore take the throw. The exception to this is the long throw, when you might wait for the specialist in your team to come across.

The throw-in
Bend your knees and arch your back while keeping good balance. Take the ball right back between the shoulder blades for maximum leverage. Release the ball as it passes in front of your head.

Penalties

Penalty kicks are becoming an ever more important source of goals in the modern game, particularly since the introduction of shoot-outs in the big tournaments. Two of the last three World Cups were decided by spot kicks. England have fared badly in this area of the game in recent years. The team went out on penalties at Italia 90, Euro 96 and France 98.

Twelve yards out, only the goalkeeper to beat, a stationary ball and no threat of a challenge: the odds are all in the kicker's favour. But perhaps the very fact that the penalty taker is expected to score is one of the reasons why so many are missed. The 'keeper is the underdog. No one expects him to make a save, so to some extent the pressure is off. Indeed, it is the players who can handle the pressure who are best suited to penalty taking. All footballers will have the technique to put the ball in the back of the net and can do it with ease in training. Not everyone has the ice-cool temperament to step up and do it when it really matters.

Some penalty takers go for sheer power and drive the ball with the instep. Newcastle's Alan Shearer has had a lot of success with this method. Other players go for greater accuracy and use the sidefoot technique instead. There is less pace on the ball, but this shouldn't matter if the placement is good. Arsenal's Thierry Henry favours this approach. If you are going to 'pass the ball into the net', remember that a low ball into the corners will pose the goalkeeper the most problems.

Make up your mind

Whatever you do, make up your mind early and stick to your decision. There are players who approach the ball with no plan. Instead, they feint to shoot, wait for the 'keeper to commit himself, then strike the ball into the empty net. This is a dangerous game. It is much safer to have a plan and keep to it.

One word of caution. These days, goalkeepers are allowed to move along the goal line before the ball is kicked. They are not allowed to come forward to narrow the angle, although many do so and get away with it! Don't allow any movement or other antics by the goalkeeper to put you off or make you change your mind. Remember, there are no good or bad penalties, only ones that go in the net and ones that don't!

Ruud van Nistelrooy of Manchester United scores a penalty against Newcastle United.

Formations

Over the years, coaches have toyed with many different formations for the ten outfield players. It seems hard to imagine now, but at one time a **2-3-5** formation dominated the game at all levels. This consisted of two full-backs, three half-backs and five forwards.

England's World Cup success.

4-2-4 was the next major development. This gave a stronger defensive unit, with two midfield players feeding the four forwards. In 1966, England tweaked this idea by pulling one of the forwards back into midfield. It was this **4-3-3** formation which brought England victory in the World Cup that year.

The midfield area was increasingly thought to be a crucial battleground. **4-4-2** was therefore a natural development of the **4-3-3** formation. Here, the two wide midfield players can break as wingers in attack and funnel back to give a solid midfield unit when the opposition is in possession. Manchester United have enjoyed a lot of success with this formation in recent years.

Three centre-backs.

More recently, some teams have started playing with three centre-backs and two wing-backs in a **3-5-2** formation. When the team is in possession, the wing-backs push forward to bolster the midfield, and even attack. When the ball is lost, they drop back into defensive positions. The problem with this system is to find players who are both solid defensively and have the flair and creativity of a midfield player.

2-3-5

4-2-4

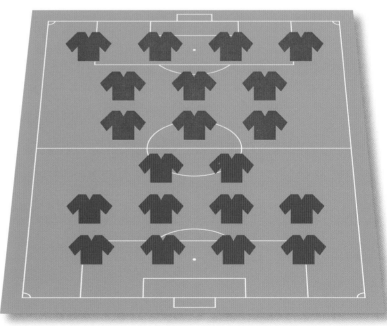

4-3-3

4-4-2

Many teams adopt an attacking formation for home games, with a more defensive set-up for away matches. Similarly, a coach might change the formation during a game if it isn't working well against particular opposition, or perhaps if a player has been sent off.

Flexibility.

Although formations and positional play are important, don't let them overcomplicate or take the fun out of the game. Also, whatever system you play, remember that it is important to attack and defend as a unit. When your team is in possession, all players should be aware of opportunities to get forward. When the opposition have the ball, everyone shares in the defensive responsibilities.

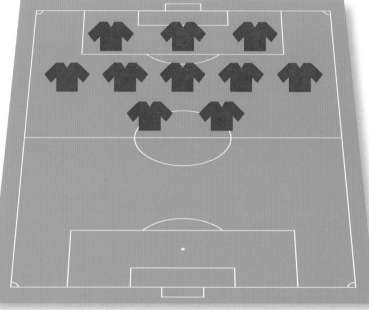

3-5-2

Lining up for kick off.